Peanut
The Wandering Elephant

Written by Robin Wettergren Bauer
Illustrated by Gau Family Studio

Dedicated to my daughters, Emily and Jenna, who encouraged me to publish this story.

It was a sunny morning and the birds were singing their cheery songs. The sound of lawn mowers could be heard throughout the neighborhood. The time was 9:00 a.m. and Mrs. Martin was off to the grocery store to buy peanuts to make her famous peanut bars for the neighborhood picnic.

Once a year in the month of June, all of the Martins' neighbors got together and ate outdoors. This was called the annual neighborhood picnic. Everyone looked forward to it. And everyone looked forward to eating Mrs. Martin's famous peanut bars.

This was Mrs. Martin's second trip to the grocery store in two days. She had already been there yesterday and bought two bags of peanuts. However, Mrs. Martin forgot to tape a note to the blue bowl that she poured the peanuts into. The note would have read: "Do not touch the peanuts. These are for my peanut bars to bring to the neighborhood picnic." But since there was no note, her family ate the peanuts.

Mr. and Mrs. Martin had two children, a boy named Josh and a girl named Abby. Josh and Abby asked to go to the grocery store with their mother.

The three of them got into the family car and drove a short distance to their local grocery store. Mr. Martin stayed behind to work in his garden. He took great pride in planting beautiful flowers and shrubs.

When Mrs. Martin and the children arrived at the store, the owner, Mr. Smith said, "Your family sure must like peanuts. You just bought two bags yesterday!"

Mrs. Martin explained that her family ate all of the peanuts because she forgot to put her "DO NOT TOUCH!" note on the blue peanut bowl.

Mr. Smith said, "Well, it's a good thing they are on sale this week."

"I guess I am lucky, Mr. Smith," said Mrs. Martin. Josh and Abby each grabbed a bag of peanuts from the shelf. They knew their mother liked to buy the peanuts with the shells, just like the ones the elephants eat at the zoo.

When they got home, Mrs. Martin walked into the kitchen and emptied the peanuts into the blue bowl. This time she wrote a note. The note read: "Do not touch the peanuts. These are for my peanut bars to bring to the neighborhood picnic."

She taped the note to the blue bowl and placed the bowl on the counter next to the kitchen window. It was such a beautiful day so she opened the window. She then left the kitchen to put some clothes into the washing machine.

Meanwhile, something mysterious was coming through the kitchen window. No one was there to take notice. It swayed back and forth and then . . . the peanuts and the note were gone!

When Mrs. Martin returned to the kitchen to prepare the peanut bars, she discovered the bowl was empty. She ran to her husband and asked if he had eaten them. Mr. Martin replied, "No honey, I have not been inside the house all morning."

"This is strange," she said. "How can a bowl of peanuts just disappear?"

Mrs. Martin had to get her peanut bars made by tomorrow and she had a lot of other things to do that day. "Well, I guess I will need to make another trip to the grocery store. I'll be right back," she said. Josh and Abby went with her to the store.

Upon arriving, they were greeted by Mr. Smith. He noticed that they were heading to the nuts and candy aisle.

"Well, Mrs. Martin, I see that my special on peanuts is a hit with you," said Mr. Smith.

"If you only knew," said Mrs. Martin. "I'm running behind schedule but will share my story with you another time." Mrs. Martin was hoping that she would eventually learn a good explanation for the missing peanuts.

This aisle contains peanuts. Please use caution if you are allergic to peanuts.

When they arrived home, Mrs. Martin walked into the kitchen and emptied the peanuts into the bowl. She wrote another note. The note read the same as last time: "Do not touch the peanuts. These are for my peanut bars to bring to the neighborhood picnic."

She taped the note to the blue bowl and placed the bowl of peanuts on the counter.

Then she left the kitchen to take the clothes out of the washing machine and put them into the dryer.

Meanwhile, something mysterious was coming through the kitchen window. It swayed back and forth and then . . . the peanuts were gone! When Mrs. Martin returned to the kitchen she found an empty bowl!

She ran to her husband and asked if he had eaten them. Mr. Martin replied: "No honey, I have been outside the entire time tending to the flower beds."

"This is strange, she said. "How can a bowl of peanuts disappear twice?"

"Well, I guess I will need to make another trip to the grocery store. I'll be right back," she said.

"I wonder what Mr. Smith from the grocery store will think?" she mumbled to herself. Once again, Josh and Abby made the trip with her to the store.

When they arrived, they were greeted by Mr. Smith.

"Well, Mrs. Martin, I'm pretty sure you have enough peanuts so what are you here for?" he asked.

"You wouldn't believe me if I told you," said Mrs. Martin.

When they got home, Mrs. Martin walked into the kitchen and emptied the peanuts into the blue bowl. She wrote yet another note: "Do not touch the peanuts. These are for my peanut bars to bring to the neighborhood picnic."

She wrote the message underlining *do not touch* three times. Then she taped the note to the bowl and left the kitchen to promptly remove the clothes from the dryer before they wrinkled.

Meanwhile, once again something mysterious came through the kitchen window. It swayed back and forth and then . . . Mrs. Martin entered the kitchen and couldn't believe what she saw! She saw what looked like an elephant outside of the kitchen window.

She ran outside to the back of the house and, sure enough, there was an elephant!

She yelled for her husband.

"What's going on?" asked Mr. Martin.

"See for yourself," said Mrs. Martin. Mr. Martin couldn't believe his eyes. Then he remembered a story he saw on the morning news. It was about an elephant that walked away from the zoo. The Martins lived two blocks from the zoo.

"This must be the elephant," Mr. Martin explained. "They said he loves peanuts. In fact, his name is Peanut!"

Mr. Martin quickly called the police, who then notified the zookeeper.

The police arrived shortly with some peanuts. They wanted to keep Peanut in the yard until the zookeeper arrived.

Peanut was a happy-go-lucky elephant. He was good natured and obedient . . . except when it came to eating peanuts, his favorite snack. The zookeeper only allowed Peanut to eat peanuts as a treat. This meant every few days. But Peanut wanted peanuts all the time!

Luckily, Peanut now had new friends that visited him often, and who loved peanuts just as much as he did.

About the author

This is Robin Wettergren Bauer's first picture book. Robin made up many bedtime stories to entertain her two daughters as they grew up. Now as a grandmother, she is telling her stories again.

Robin was born and raised in St. Peter, Minnesota (a city known for its *little bit of heaven*). She now resides in Victoria, Minnesota.

CPSIA information can be obtained at www.ICGtesting.com
Printed in the USA
LVIW01n0133180116
471116LV00001B/1

* 9 7 8 1 6 3 3 1 8 2 2 8 8 *